Fable… Af…

Timothy Knapman

Illustrated by
Linda Selby
Hannah Firmin

CONTENTS

OXFORD
UNIVERSITY PRESS

Dear Reader,

Nobody likes being told what to do all the time. So how do you teach people the important lessons we all have to learn? One way is to make the lessons fun. You can turn them into a special kind of story, called a 'fable'.

These fables all come from Africa.

I hope you enjoy them!

Timothy Knapman

The Tortoise and the Baboon

A fable from Southern Africa

Baboon thought it was funny to play tricks on people. One afternoon, he saw Tortoise walking along. Tortoise was going so slowly that he gave Baboon an idea.

'My dear old friend,' said Baboon. 'Goodness me, you're looking thin!'

'That's because I couldn't find anything to eat today,' said Tortoise gloomily.

‘Then you must come and have supper with me,’ said Baboon. ‘I’ve got plenty of food and I’m a very good cook. Giraffe is always coming over and you know what a fussy eater he is.’

‘Thank you, Baboon,’ said Tortoise.

Baboon scampered off to get things ready.

It took poor Tortoise ages to get to Baboon's home. The path was long and knobbly and a lot of it was uphill.

More than once Tortoise thought about giving up. Then he remembered the food Baboon had promised him and that gave him the strength to go on.

‘That wasn’t me,’ said Baby Warthog. ‘It was that lion up there!’

Sure enough, a lion was hanging upside down from the tree above them. He had been caught in a trap.

'Please,' said Lion, 'let me down. I've been up here for three days and I think I've gone peculiar.'

'How silly do you think we are?' said Mr Warthog. 'If we let you down, you'll eat us!'

'I promise I won't!' pleaded Lion. 'I'm so weak from lack of food I'm as harmless as a kitten.'

So the Warthogs undid the trap and set Lion free.

‘Thank you so much,’ said Lion. ‘Dear Mr Warthog, sweet Mrs Warthog and lovely, delicious, good-enough-to-eat Baby Warthog, I am so grateful, I could just gobble you up!’

Mrs Warthog didn’t like the sound of that. She didn’t like the way Lion was looking at Baby Warthog and licking his lips either.

So, very quickly, she said, 'How on earth did you get caught in this trap?'

'I was just wandering along, minding my own business,' said Lion, 'when I put my paw here,' and Lion put his paw back into the trap to show them. 'Then the rope went tight, and the next thing I knew I was hanging upside down from that tree.'

'Like this?' said Mrs Warthog, and she pulled hard so that the rope went tight and Lion was once again hanging upside down from the tree.

'What did you do that for?' said Lion.

'My family and I set you free,' said Mrs Warthog, 'and you were going to thank us by eating Baby Warthog here! What an ungrateful scoundrel you are.'

The Warthogs turned their backs and walked away with their noses in the air.

Lion hung upside down like that for another three days until Grass Mouse came by.

'Excuse me,' said Lion, who was now so weak from lack of food that his voice was just a whisper. 'Would you please be kind enough to help me down? I promise I won't hurt you.'

Grass Mouse's mother had told him to steer clear of lions, but she had also said that he should always help fellow creatures in trouble.

'All right then,' said Grass Mouse. He scampered up the tree and with his sharp front teeth he gnawed through the rope that was holding Lion.

'Thank you so much,' said Lion when he was back on solid ground.

Lion wasn't going to make the same mistake twice, so instead of thinking about eating Grass Mouse, he promised to help him whenever he was in trouble.

Moral of the tale

Always be grateful when people help you.

The Hungry Hyena

A fable from Southern Africa

Hyena hadn't eaten for a week and his stomach was making the most extraordinary noises.

He watched the other animals going by, with their shiny eyes and their glossy coats and felt so sorry for himself.

'Go on, just one more,' said Jackal. 'Hurry, though. Soon it'll be sunrise and the men will be on their way.'

They were just waddling over to the hole in the fence when Jackal saw a particularly tasty looking goat.

'What are you doing?' said Hyena.

'One bite can't do any harm,' replied Jackal.

'I thought you said–'

Too late! Jackal was so tempted that he ignored his own advice and sank his teeth into the goat's shoulder.

The goat gave a terrible shriek and at once the dogs started barking.

'Oops!' said Jackal. 'Quick! Before the men get here!'

The two of them dashed over to the hole in the fence. Jackal just about wriggled through, but Hyena was now so large with all the food he had eaten, he got stuck.

'Help!' cried Hyena.

'Sorry, chum,' said Jackal. 'It's what I planned all along. The men will be so busy punishing you, they'll never catch me!' He raced off as fast as he could go.

Hyena struggled with all his might, but it was no good. He was trapped. The men were coming and they were very cross.

As he curled up later, all alone and miserable, Hyena had quite forgotten the delicious feast he'd enjoyed only a few hours before.

He swore he'd be more careful when he chose his friends in future.

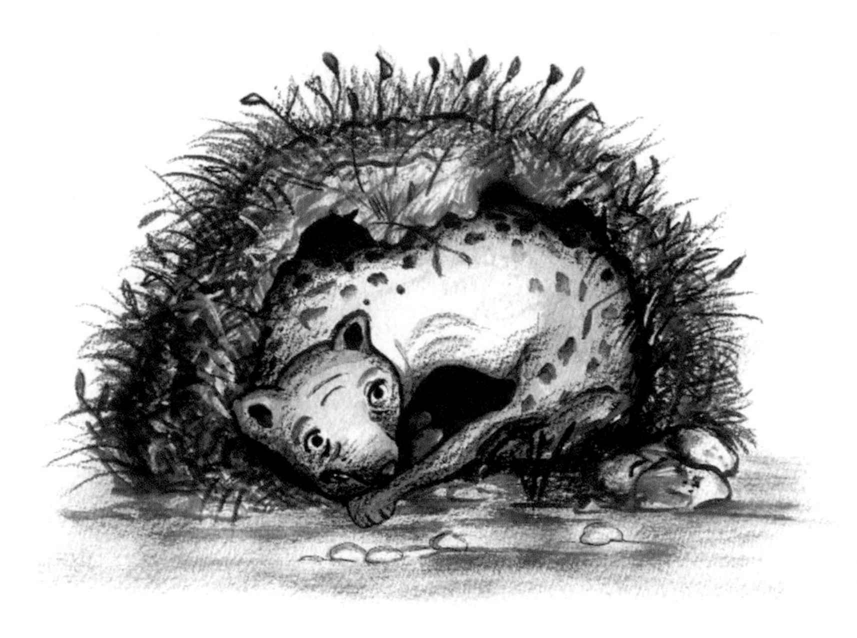

Moral of the tale

Beware of friends you cannot trust.

The Bag of Salt

A fable from East/Central Africa

Salt was very hard to come by where Tortoise lived so he went to get some from his brother, who had plenty to spare.

Tortoise was on his way home again, dragging the salt behind him in a little bag, when he heard a thump and found he couldn't go any further.

He looked round and saw a great big lizard sitting on the bag.

‘Would you please get off my bag of salt?’ said Tortoise.

‘*Your* bag of salt?’ said Lizard. ‘I saw this bag of salt just lying on the road and I jumped on it and claimed it. That makes it mine, not yours!’

‘Don’t be so silly,’ said Tortoise, but Lizard wouldn’t budge.

The elders were very impressed by the wisdom and justice of Lizard's argument and decided that the bag of salt should be divided equally between him and Tortoise.

Lizard made sure that he got the bottom half of the bag, so Tortoise's share just spilled out onto the floor.

'I'm very cut up about this, you know,' laughed Lizard as Tortoise stormed off.

Tortoise spent days plotting his revenge and then went looking for Lizard. He found him lying in the road, lazily eating insects.

Tortoise climbed up on Lizard's back and cried out, 'Look what I've found!'

‘What are you doing?’ asked Lizard.

‘I saw this lizard lying in the road and I jumped on it. That makes it mine,’ said Tortoise. He wouldn’t budge until Lizard agreed to go to the elders and let them decide the matter.

'If we're going to be fair, we ought to give the same decision as we did last time,' they said. 'So we decree that the lizard should be divided equally between you.'

'What?' said Lizard, who knew he'd been caught out.

'Don't tell me,' said Tortoise, 'you're very cut up about this, aren't you?'

Moral of the tale

Don't take what isn't yours.

Stronger than the Lion

A fable from Southern Africa

Lion was really getting on everyone's nerves.

'I am the king of the jungle!' he'd roar at anyone who'd listen. 'The best of beasts! The top banana! My word, you're lucky that I'm even *talking* to you!'

The rest of the animals didn't *feel* very lucky, and they would have told Lion as much if only they hadn't been so frightened of him.

All?

Well, not quite.

Hare could run faster than Lion so he wasn't afraid of him. One day, after Lion had been especially boastful and annoying, Hare said, 'Actually, there is one creature I know who is stronger than you.'

The other animals gasped. Someone had been brave enough to disagree with Lion!

'Oh really?' snorted Lion. 'And who is that, pray?'

'I'll show you if you like,' said Hare. 'Come with me.'

Hare took Lion to a tumbledown old house, way out in the middle of nowhere.

'He's in there,' he said.

Despite himself, Lion felt a little anxious as he padded inside. He was even more anxious when Hare locked the door behind him. He explored the whole place and eventually called out, 'This house is empty. Where is this terrifying creature that is even stronger than me?'

'Oh, he'll be along,' said Hare. 'Don't you worry.'

Hare came back the next day and knocked at the door.

'Has he come yet, Lion?' he asked.

'No, he hasn't,' roared Lion. 'If this is some kind of trick, I will make you regret it, I promise!'

'It's no trick,' said Hare.

A whole week went by before Hare went back to the house again.

'Well, Lion?' he asked. 'Has your visitor been yet?'

This time there was no angry roar. Instead, Lion said 'No,' in a parched croak.

Hare unlocked the door and went in. He found the once powerful Lion stretched out on the floor, so thin that he was little more than a skeleton wrapped in a skin.

'Lion, you fibber!' said Hare. 'The creature that is stronger than you has come after all.'

'Really?' said Lion. With the last of his strength, he lifted his head and looked around. 'Who is he?'

'Hunger,' said Hare.

Moral of the tale

There is always something stronger than you.